This book belongs to:

_____

D1022009

Contents

Cover illustration by Michael Charlton

A catalogue record for this book is available
from the British Library

Published by Ladybird Books Ltd
A subsidiary of the Penguin Group
A Pearson Company
© LADYBIRD BOOKS LTD MCMXCVII

LADYBIRD and the device of a Ladybird are trademarks of
Ladybird Books Ltd Loughborough Leicestershire UK

Double trouble

written by Alan MacDonald
illustrated by Ann Kronheimer

Sam's Burger Bar made the best burgers in town. Big and juicy in a soft white bun: cheese burgers, vegetable burgers and hamburgers. But best of all were 'Sam's Double Trouble Burgers' for really big eaters. Sam always kept his window open, so the smell of burgers drifted down the street.

4

People were suddenly very hungry
and soon they found themselves
at Sam's counter.

"Hungry?" said Sam.

"Very," they said.

"One Double Trouble Burger coming
right up," said Sam.

Sam's Burger Bar was always busy.
Two of Sam's customers came
every day. Their names were Slow Joe
and the Ketchup Kid. They both liked
burgers, but they didn't like each other.

One day Slow Joe
was sitting at his
usual table. Sam brought
him a burger. Slow Joe liked
his burgers plain. No cheese,
no ketchup, no onion. He chewed
slowly. He looked up as the Ketchup Kid
came into the bar.

7

The Ketchup Kid liked burgers with cheese and onion. Most of all he liked tomato ketchup. Lots of it. It oozed out of the sides of the burger and onto his plate. The Ketchup Kid licked his lips.

Slow Joe stared across at him in disgust. The Ketchup Kid stared back and pulled a face.

Sam started to put his best plates under the counter. There was trouble in the air.

Slow Joe finished eating.
He nodded to Sam.

"Another Double Trouble Burger, Sam.
No extras."

"Make that two Double Trouble Burgers,"
said the Ketchup Kid.
"One with all the extras."

Sam took them their burgers.
But he was in too much of a hurry.

"There's cheese and onion on this
burger," grumbled Slow Joe.

"And there's nothing on mine," said the Ketchup Kid.

"Oh, no," thought Sam. "I must have mixed them up."

The Ketchup Kid walked over
to Slow Joe's table.

"That's my burger you've got there,
Slow Joe."

"And that's mine, Ketchup Kid."

The Ketchup Kid smiled
and squeezed ketchup
on both burgers.
Slow Joe got to his feet.
He looked mad.

"I don't like ketchup,"
he said.

Sam got down under the counter.
There was going to be a showdown.
The other customers ran for the door.
Only one hungry little girl stayed behind
to watch.

13

Slow Joe and the Ketchup Kid stood back to back. They had ketchup bottles in each hand. Slowly, they started to walk.

One… two… three…

Ten paces, then they would turn and squeeze.

Sam couldn't bear to watch.

He was thinking of the mess.

Slow Joe spun round. So did the Ketchup Kid. They got ready to squeeze their ketchup. But just at that moment the little girl burped.

Slow Joe and the Ketchup Kid stared. Their Double Trouble Burgers had gone. In their place sat two empty plates and the little girl licking her lips.

They both went over to her table.

"Hey, little girl. What's your name?" asked Slow Joe.

"They call me Quick Kate," she said.

"Why, because you're quick on the draw?" asked the Ketchup Kid.

"No, because I'm quick out the door," said the little girl.
And with that, she was gone.

Slow Joe and the Ketchup Kid looked at each other.

They felt very silly... and hungry.

"Sam..." they said.

"Coming right up," said Sam.

Picking
teams

written by Colin Pearce
illustrated by Michael Charlton

On Saturdays, Jim takes us
to play football.

Ben and Stefan pick teams because they're the biggest.

Ben picks Billy Lock because they've been best friends for ever and ever.

Stefan picks Paddy Brown because he's tall and he can jump and he's good in goal.

But no one ever picks me.

Ben picks my big brother, Harry,
because he's the best kicker in
our street.

Stefan picks Beth Taylor because
she can run fast and I think
he likes her.

But no one ever picks me.

Ben picks Charlie Johnson because he's got the best football boots.

Stefan picks Olly King because he's strong and he tackles anyone and he never cares when it hurts.

They divide up the players
so both sides are equal.
But no one ever picks me.

"What about Jake?" says Paddy.

"Oh… he can be reserve.
Sit over there, Jake, and wait until
you're called," said Ben.

"Hello, Jake," said Jim.
"Not playing?"

"They've picked teams,
but they didn't pick me."

"Good," said Jim.
"I need you to be referee
because you're the fairest."
And he gave me a whistle.

I blew the whistle when Paddy
brought Charlie down
with his big feet…

and I blew it when
Stefan scored a goal
over Billy's head.

And when Harry shouted "Penalty!"
after Beth tackled him,
I didn't blow it. I yelled, "Play on!"

And when the game was over
I blew it long and loud,
and Stefan's team were the
winners – one-nil.

"Great game," said Jim.
"Great ref. Will you be ref
next Saturday, Jake?"

Jokes, jokes, jokes!

illustrated by David Pattison

What do baby snakes
play with?

Rattlesnakes!

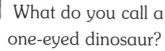

What do you get if you cross
a centipede with a parrot?

A walkie-talkie!

What do you call a
one-eyed dinosaur?

Do-you-think-he-saurus!

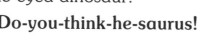

What do you call a one-eyed
dinosaur's dog?

Do-you-think-he-saurus Rex!

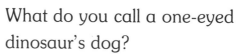

Why do cows have cowbells?
Because their horns don't work!

 Knock, knock **Who's there?**
Granny **Granny who?**

Knock, knock **Who's there?**
Granny **Granny who?**

Knock, knock **Who's there?**
Granny **Granny who?**

Knock, knock **Who's there?**
Aunt **Aunt who?**

Aunt you glad all those
grannies have gone!

Learning to read with this book

Special features

Picking teams and other stories is ideal for early independent reading. It includes:

• two longer stories to build stamina.

• jokes for enjoyable reading – and a good laugh to share.

Planned to help your child to develop his reading by:

• practising a variety of reading techniques such as recognising frequently used words on sight, being able to read words with similar spelling patterns (eg, bun/spun), and the use of letter-sound clues.

• using rhyme to improve memory.

• including illustrations that make reading even more enjoyable.

Read with Ladybird...

is specially designed to help your child learn to read. It will complement all the methods used in schools.

Parents took part in extensive research to ensure that **Read with Ladybird** would help your child to:

- take the first steps in reading
- improve early reading progress
- gain confidence in new-found abilities.

The research highlighted that the most important qualities in helping children to read were that:

- books should be fun – children have enough 'hard work' at school
- books should be colourful and exciting
- stories should be up to date and about everyday experiences
- repetition and rhyme are especially important in boosting a child's reading ability.

The stories and rhymes introduce the 100 words most frequently used in reading and writing.

These 100 key words actually make up half the words we use in speech and reading.

The three levels of **Read with Ladybird** consist of 22 books, taking your child from two words per page to 600-word stories.

Read with Ladybird will help your child to master the basic reading skills so vital in everyday life.

Ladybird have successfully published reading schemes and programmes for the last 50 years. Using this experience and the latest research, **Read with Ladybird** has been produced to give all children the head start they deserve.